STERLING and the distinctive Sterling logo are registered trademarks of Sterling Publishing Co., Inc.

Library of Congress Cataloging-in-Publication Data
Wilhelm, Hans, 1945-
Mother Goose on the loose / illustrated by Hans Wilhelm.
p. cm.
"Old Mother Goose, when she wanted to wander, would ride through the air on a very fine gander."
Summary: A collection of traditional rhymes accompanied by illustrations of various animals celebrating the seasons.
ISBN 978-1-4027-6398-4
1. Nursery rhymes. 2. Children's poetry. [1. Nursery rhymes.] I. Title.
PZ8.3.W664Mo 2009
398.8--dc22

2008041311

2 4 6 8 10 9 7 5 3 1

Published in 2009 by Sterling Publishing Co., Inc.

Original edition of this book published in 1989 by Sterling Publishing Co., Inc.

387 Park Avenue South, New York, NY 10016
Distributed in Canada by Sterling Publishing
c/o Canadian Manda Group, 165 Dufferin Street
Toronto, Ontario, Canada M6K 3H6
Distributed in the United Kingdom by GMC Distribution Services
Castle Place, 166 High Street, Lewes, East Sussex, England BN7 1XU
Distributed in Australia by Capricorn Link (Australia) Pty. Ltd.
P.O. Box 704, Windsor, NSW 2756, Australia

Printed in China

Sterling ISBN 978-1-4027-6398-4

For information about custom editions, special sales, premium and corporate purchases, please contact Sterling Special Sales Department at 800-805-5489 or specialsales@sterlingpublishing.com.

Old Mother Goose,
when she wanted to wander,
would ride through the air
on a very fine gander.

Mother Goose *on the* Loose

Illustrated by Hans Wilhelm

STERLING
New York / London

January brings the snow,
makes our feet and fingers glow.

London Bridge is falling down,
falling down, falling down.
London Bridge is falling down,
my fair lady.

Curly Locks, Curly Locks,
will you be mine?
You shall not wash dishes
not yet feed the swine,

but sit on a cushion
and sew a fine seam,
and feed upon strawberries,
sugar, and cream.

Jack be nimble,
Jack be quick,
Jack jump over
the candlestick.

February brings the rain,
thaws the frozen lake again.

Little Polly Flinders
sat among the cinders,
warming her pretty little toes.
Her mother came and caught her
and shouted at her daughter
for spoiling her nice new clothes.

March brings breezes, loud and shrill,
to stir the dancing daffodil.

Daffy-down-dilly has come up to town
in a yellow petticoat and a green gown.

Rain, rain, go away.
Come again another day.

As the days grow longer,
the storms grow stronger.

April brings the primrose sweet,
scatters daisies at our feet.

Yankee Doodle came to town,
riding on a pony.
He stuck a feather in his cap
and called it Macaroni.

Rain on the green grass
and rain on the tree.
Rain on the house top,
but not on me.

A sunshiny shower
won't last half an hour.

Mary, Mary, quite contrary,
how does your garden grow?
With silver bells
and cockleshells
and pretty maids all in a row.

May brings flocks of pretty lambs,
skipping by their fleecy dams.

Ring-a-ring o' roses,
a pocket full of posies.
A-tishoo! A-tishoo!
We all fall down!

Baa, baa, black sheep,
have you any wool?
Yes, sir, yes, sir,
three bags full.
One for the master,
and one for the dame,
and one for the little boy
who lives down the lane.

Cock-a-doodle-doo!
My dame has lost her shoe.
My master's lost his fiddlestick
and knows not what to do.

June brings tulips, lilies, roses,
fills the children's hands with posies.

Mary had a little lamb,
its fleece was white as snow,
and everywhere that Mary went
the lamb was sure to go.
It followed her to school one day
which was against the rule.
It made the children laugh and play
to see a lamb at school.

Swan swam over the sea.
Swim, swan, swim!
Swan swam back again.
Well swum, swan!

Old King Cole was a merry old soul,
and a merry old soul was he.
He called for his pipe
and he called for his bowl
and he called for his fiddlers three.

Every fiddler, he had a fiddle,
and a very fine fiddle had he.
Twee tweedle dee, tweedle dee, went the fiddlers.
Oh, there's none so rare as can compare
with King Cole and his fiddlers three.

Hot July brings cooling showers,
apricots, and gillyflowers.

I'm the king of the castle.
Get down, you dirty rascal!

Mother, may I go out to swim?
Yes, my darling daughter.
Hang your clothes on a hickory limb
and don't go near the water.

Rub-a-dub-dub,
Three men in a tub,
and who do you think
they be?
The butcher, the baker,
the candlestick maker;
they all jumped out
of a rotten potato.
Turn 'em out,
knaves all three!

August brings the sheaves of corn,
then the harvest time is borne.

Hickory, dickory, dock.
the mouse ran up the clock.
The clock struck one,
the mouse ran down.
Hickory, dickory, dock.

Little Miss Muffet
sat on a tuffet,
eating her curds and whey.
There came a big spider,
who sat down beside her
and frightened Miss Muffet away.

Little Boy Blue,
come blow your horn.
The sheep's in the meadow,
the cow's in the corn,
but where is the boy
who looks after the sheep?
He's under the haystack,
fast asleep.
Will you wake him?
No, not I, for if I do,
he's sure to cry.

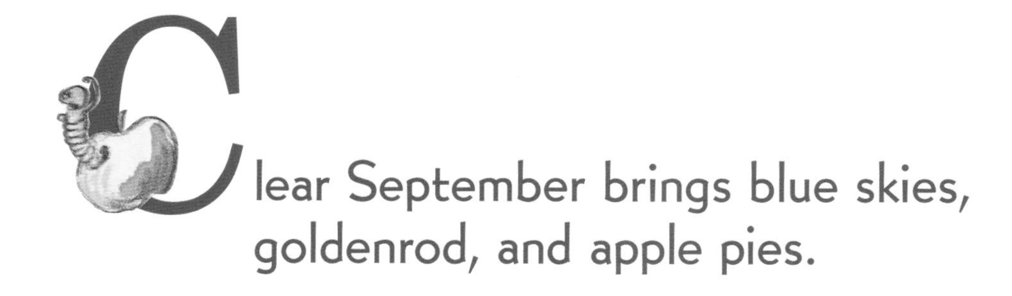

Clear September brings blue skies,
goldenrod, and apple pies.

An apple a day
keeps the doctor away.

Jack Sprat could eat no fat.
His wife could eat no lean.
And so betwixt the both of them,
they licked the platter clean.

As I went up the apple tree,
all the apples fell on me.
Bake a pudding, bake a pie,
did you ever tell a lie?
Yes, I did, and many times.
O-U-T, out goes she,
right in the middle of the deep blue sea.

Fresh October brings the pheasant,
then to gather nuts is pleasant.

Bat, bat, come under my hat
and I'll give you a slice of bacon.
And when I bake, I'll give you a cake,
if I am not mistaken.

Hey diddle diddle,
the cat and the fiddle,
the cow jumped over the moon.

The little dog laughed
to see such sport,
and the dish ran away
with the spoon.

Dull November brings the blast,
makes the leaves go whirling past.

Hush-a-bye, baby, on the tree top.
When the wind blows, the cradle will rock.
When the bough breaks, the cradle will fall.
Down will come baby, cradle and all.

There was an old woman
who lived in a shoe.
She had so many children,
she didn't know what to do.
She gave them some broth
without any bread,
and kissed them all softly
and sent them to bed.

Chill December brings the sleet,
blazing fire, and Christmas treat.

Christmas comes
but once a year,
and when it comes,
it brings good cheer.